Your Heart,
My Sky

Also by Margarita Engle

also available in Spanish

Enchanted Air:
*Two Cultures, Two Wings: A Memoir**

The Firefly Letters:
A Suffragette's Journey to Cuba

Forest World*

Hurricane Dancers:
The First Caribbean Pirate Shipwreck

Jazz Owls:
A Novel of the Zoot Suit Riots

The Lightning Dreamer:
Cuba's Greatest Abolitionist

Lion Island:
*Cuba's Warrior of Words**

The Poet Slave of Cuba:
A Biography of Juan Francisco Manzano

Silver People:
Voices from the Panama Canal

Soaring Earth:
*A Companion Memoir to Enchanted Air**

The Surrender Tree:
*Poems of Cuba's Struggle for Freedom**

Tropical Secrets:
Holocaust Refugees in Cuba

The Wild Book

With a Star in My Hand:
*Rubén Darío, Poetry Hero **

LOVE IN A TIME OF HUNGER

YOUR
Heart
MY
Sky

MARGARITA ENGLE

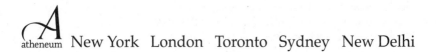

atheneum   New York   London   Toronto   Sydney   New Delhi

An imprint of Simon & Schuster Children's Publishing Division
1230 Avenue of the Americas, New York, New York 10020

Atheneum logo is a trademark of Simon & Schuster, Inc.

For information about special discounts for bulk purchases, please contact Simon & Schuster Special Sales at 1-866-506-1949 or business@simonandschuster.com.

The Simon & Schuster Speakers Bureau can bring authors to your live event. For more information or to book an event, contact the Simon & Schuster Speakers Bureau at 1-866-248-3049 or visit our website at www.simonspeakers.com.

The text for this book was set in Palatino.
Manufactured in the United States of America

10 9 8 7 6 5 4 3 2

Library of Congress Cataloging-in-Publication Data
Names: Engle, Margarita, author.
Title: Your heart, my sky : love in the time of hunger / Margarita Engle. Description: First edition. | New York : Atheneum Books for Young Readers, [2021] | Audience: Ages 12 up. | Audience: Grades 7–9. | Summary: In Cuba's "special period in times of peace" of 1991, Liana and Amado find love after their severe hunger gives both courage to risk government retribution by skipping a summer of labor to seek food. Told in their two voices plus that of the stray dog that brought them together.
Identifiers: LCCN 2020012225 | ISBN 9781534464964 (hardcover) | ISBN 9781534464988 (eBook)
Subjects: CYAC: Starvation—Fiction. | Dogs—Fiction. | Love—Fiction. | Family life—Cuba—Fiction. | Cuba—History—20th century—Fiction.
Classification: LCC PZ7.5.E54 You 2021 | DDC [Fic]—dc23
LC record available at https://lccn.loc.gov/2020012225

Para los balseros
y los que se quedaron

Your Heart,
My Sky

Cuba es tu corazón, Cuba es mi cielo,
Cuba en tu libro mi palabra sea.

Cuba is your heart, Cuba is my sky,
In your book, Cuba is my word.

—José Martí,
from "Cuba nos une" (*"Cuba Unites Us"*)

Island of Cuba
Summer 1991

Imagine a year when food suddenly vanishes.
It's the beginning of a decade known as
el período especial en tiempos de paz—
the special period in times of peace.

> Hunger drives tens of thousands
> > into the ferocious blue sea
> > > on fragile rafts.

Hunger teaches others how to cling to red soil
and green fields, reinventing ancient ways
to survive.

Hunger
helps lonely beings
sing.

Emptiness
Liana, age 14

Haunted belly,
the memory of food
so vivid.

We're ordered to call this plunging shock of hunger
el período especial en tiempos de paz—
the special period in times of peace—
meaning warlike sacrifices
with hope as our only defensive weapon.

I obey the government's instructions
for referring to an alarming absence of food,
even though official words always
seem tricky.

Special, I repeat,
meaning ravenous.

Peace, I recite,
imagining meat.

Global Games
Liana

In just a few weeks, athletes from many nations
will arrive on our isolated isla, to compete
in los Juegos panamericanos.

I close my eyes and picture airplanes landing,
foreigners emerging to play fútbol, béisbol,
and básquetbol tournaments, all the world
watching the Pan American Games on televisions
in well-fed lands
far away.

I imagine the kitchens in those homes.
Full refrigerators and a fragrance of cooking . . .

Our quiet town is remote, so the global games
in Havana
might pass
without any travelers
ever finding us.

No witnesses.
We are like an outer isle
        off the shore of another island.

                                    Forgotten.

But what if a few sports fans do show up?
We're not allowed to talk to foreigners,
but I, for one, would love to break official rules
just to see how fairness feels.
Curiosity
is stronger
than fear.

Wondering about the World
Liana

How do foreigners think,
what do they believe,
what do they
                    eat?

What if they see
how emaciated we are?

Won't they fly home
and come back with food
to share?

/

The History of Our Hunger
Liana

According to legends told by old folks,
this is how emptiness swallowed us:
Nearly thirty years ago, the US refused
to trade with Cuba, so we fell into the bear hug
of Russia, until a few months ago, when suddenly
the Soviet Union began to crumble like a sandcastle,
leaving

      us

          abandoned.

No more subsidies, bribes, or rewards.
Now, with tourists from all over the world
due to arrive for global games, our food rations
are slashed to create an illusion of plenty
at hotel banquets, in restaurants that we

          are not permitted

          to enter.

My parents quietly call it tourist apartheid.
Everything for outsiders.

          Nothing for islanders.

Sharing Sugar
Liana

A sandy brown dog approaches me.
He's lean and muscular, with sensitive eyes
and an attentive nose, sniffing hot air
to inhale
my closeness.

I reach and touch, needing friendship.
All I have to offer is a sip of sweetened water,
because sugar is the only food in our kitchen
abundant enough to share.

The rest of my family's rations—rice, beans, flour—
are so stingy that we run out halfway through
each month, forcing us to starve
or scrounge
like beggars.

I feel so weak
from this diet of azúcar
that my body seems to float,
while my mind   explores. . . .

Plans and Fantasies
Liana

Three simple decisions are needed today.
Uno:
Can I keep the wild-looking dog?

Dos:
Am I brave enough to skip la escuela al campo—
school in the countryside—
a summer of forced so-called-volunteer farm labor
that always feels like teenage slavery?
Anyone who doesn't show up
won't stand a chance of getting into college
or being assigned to a tolerable job, because
the government controls us so completely
that even our careers are assigned.

Tres:
What can I find to gobble
for breakfast, lunch, or supper?
There's no point wishing for all three meals.
Eating until I'm full even once per day would be
sheer
             ecstasy!

At Night, the Mind Feels Nourished
Liana

The first and second decisions are urgent:
I'll have to find a way to feed the lean dog,
and to stay sane I need to dodge the hideous
work camps, even though my family might suffer
the revenge of a judgmental government,
and we could be shunned by neighbors
if we're labeled
as traitors.

So I'll make myself seem lazy, but at least
there will be a chance to conserve my energy,
so that I can spend every minute searching for food.

Together, the dog and I fall asleep
dreaming of protein.
Milk.
Meat.
Eggs.
Treasures I have not tasted
all year.

Monstrous
Liana

Which is worse,
starvation or prison?

Stealing food is dangerous.
Roadside bananas belong to the government.
So do lobsters in the sea, and cattle that roam
rough green pastures.

The penalty for killing a cow
is thirty years in prison.

Barriga llena, corazón contento.
Full belly, happy heart—
unless you happen to be an islander
during this special period of peaceful desperation,
when emptiness makes me feel like a beast
with a hollow belly.
No heart
at all.

Serenade
Liana

With the eager dog at my side
I roam every beach,
peering
into sand
and water
as we seek
edible creatures.

When the dog begins to sing
his voice is eerie, echoing like the howl
of a werewolf in an old movie, but livelier,
more musical,
a song of hope,
not despair.

Wild
The singing dog, age unknown

The dog is acutely aware of human hunger.
Otherwise, he might have stayed
alone in the wilderness forever,
instead of following a pungent scent-trail of time
back and forth
between lonely mountains
and forgotten towns.

He's the only survivor from a long-lost era
when all canines chanted rhymes instead of barking.

Silent while hunting,
they yowled like four-legged poets
as soon as a meal of shellfish, lizards, or rodents
was captured
and swallowed.

Now, the dog feels like he's made of memories
wrapped up in a nest of fur
and sound.

Plea
Liana

My name means jungle vine,
a plant that grows tangled like prayers.

Protein is my most urgent wish,
but I've started pleading for a guardian angel, too,
even though faith has been forbidden for so long
that if anyone
hears me
secretly
speaking
to heaven,
I'll be treated
like an outlaw.

Response

Liana

The dog comforts me.
There's something sacred
about his musical nature.

He sings.
I listen.

Maybe companionship
is the only answer
to all prayers.

Local Games
Liana

The singing dog helps me find
enough odd-tasting protein
to regain a bit of hope.

I never imagined that I would swallow
raw sea creatures so eagerly, but I do,
and now I feel daring, bold,
body and soul
both almost full.

In a spirit of celebration, I play
with the neighborhood's smallest children.
Cuatro esquinas. Street baseball.
Pon. Hopscotch.
Bolas. Marbles.
Yaquis. Jacks.
El gato y el ratón. Cat and rat.
El lobo y los corderos. Wolf and lambs.

I remember all the English translations
I learned from an old dictionary
hidden at the back of my mother's
cluttered bookshelf.

When I was little, my favorite game
was la vuelta al tronco, which I played
with my twin brothers, all three of us
spinning around a tree trunk,
then turning to twirl
the other way
until
finally
we
grew
dizzy
and
collapsed
like broken twigs.

So I try it now, with the eager dog
and a half dozen shrieking children
all tumbling over each other
in an effort
to race,
even though
there are no prizes,
just laughter.

Until this moment
the sorrow of hunger
has made me forget
that daily life can be
a twisting
spinning
whirlwind
of
sheer
joy!

The Next Morning
Liana

My parents scold me for staying home
instead of going with my brothers to la escuela
al campo, but their anger passes quickly,
and then they hug me, pretending it's not
a burden to have one more person to feed
all summer, along with this unexpected
canine guest
my four-legged angel
a skinny, ravenous beast
of hope.

What will we eat, dog?
Have I imagined you?
Are you real?

Can hunger make a sane girl feel
crazed enough to hallucinate
an imaginary
four-legged
friend?

The Marvels of Reality
The singing dog

He knows he is real.
He exhales forcefully before each inhaled puff.
Huff! Sniff. It's the pattern of air breathed by all
his ancestors. The fragrance of time is everywhere,
so he is selective as he chooses seconds,
minutes, hours,
centuries. . . .

Following airborne aromas, he leads the girl
toward her scented future,
each adventure ending with the edible prize
of something nutritious,
a discarded fish head, plump tree rat,
or jumping bullfrog.

The dog knows that trusting all these strange smells
will be his only way to feel strong enough for music.

Glimpse
Amado, age 15

I'm the only boy in this entire town
who did not go to the sugar fields
for a summer of oppressive labor.

Everyone knows it's more mandatory
than voluntary, at least in the sense
of becoming an outcast if you refuse,
losing all privileges, forfeiting college,
losing hope for a future of education
and respect.

So I wander alone now, observing, listening,
trying to discover rare sources of food, ration lines
that lead to bread or coffee, instead of the usual
slice of aching
disappointment.

All my friends left yesterday
on flatbed army trucks, carted like cattle.
I don't expect to see any teenagers in town,
so I'm surprised when I spot a girl I've noticed
many times, even though I've never
been brave enough to speak to her.

Close to her side, a foxlike animal
lopes casually, fearless in the presence
of hungry strangers.

Doesn't the wild-looking dog understand
that most of us are ravenous enough
to lose our sense of guilt?

Cats have disappeared
and dogs are vanishing too,
abandoned, gone feral,
or worse—devoured, the meat
described as pork or rabbit. . . .

No one can afford to feed a pet.
We can barely take care of ourselves.
Some would eat this creature just to fill
the agony of a hollow belly
and vanishing conscience.

Glance
Liana

The tall boy who gazes at me
is even skinnier than the rest of us.

He's skeletal but appealing
in a days-on-earth-are-numbered
sort of way.

He must be courageous
to skip la escuela al campo!

As soon as that admiring thought
flashes across my mind, I realize that
I'm brave too.

Sometimes it takes a clear view
     of someone else
before I can see my own
     unexpected self.

Mirror
Amado

The girl's curious eyes make me want
to go home and look at myself
in an effort to see what she perceives:
Height.
Emaciation.
Bones barely concealed
by skin, my face the same deep brown
as this old mirror's scratched
mahogany frame.

The girl has no way to know that I crave
so much more than food—I need freedom
to speak out, demanding my right
to reject silence.

My older brother is already in prison
for the same crime that I plan to commit—
evading the draft by staying away on the day
when I'm ordered to report for military duty.

Our grandfather fought in Bolivia,
our father in Nicaragua and Angola,
enough bloodshed to leave both of us
unwilling to join future battles.

I glare at the mirror.
Wavy patches.
Blurry streaks.
As if I'm already
fading away
in a prison cell.

What if I don't have the courage
to keep the pact that I made with my brother,
speaking up, explaining to the government
why we need to choose peace?

But this country is not at war right now,
unless you count our constant struggle
against hunger.

Maybe I should let myself be trained to kill,
become a soldier, gun-wielding, violent,
a dangerous stranger, no longer
me.

Reflection

Liana

The dog and I crouch,
watching ourselves
in a shallow tide pool,
shimmery bronze faces
rippling as we hover
above pink anemones
and purple sea urchins.

We gobble
odd-shaped creatures
raw, then glance
at ourselves again,
the dog's hair short and straight,
mine long, wet, and twining
in dark ringlets like tendrils or seaweed.

Our eyes resemble four sleek black planets
floating in the tide pool's
miniature galaxy.

Do canines understand mirror images,
or can they only recognize themselves
by smell?

I'll never know, unless I learn
the ancient language of dog songs.

After a while, we rise and climb
the steep, brightly flowered hills of town,
passing old houses with climbing vines
that enclose wide-open windows and doors,
an invitation for the sea breeze, doves,
butterflies, wasps,
perhaps also thieves. . . .

At home in my kitchen,
I check the refrigerator,
finding it empty as usual.

No electricity either.
Just invisible
wishes.

Herding Teenagers
The singing dog

If he can somehow manage to urge them
toward each other, then neither one will feel
so completely alone, and his unusual instincts
tell him that these two are so perfectly
right for each other that if he fails
to meet his natural goal they will wander
like detached spirits, souls just as starved
as bodies. . . .

The last time a singing dog worked at matchmaking
was in the human year 1519, when a violent pirate
named Hernán Cortés had stolen a ship and anchored
on the island's southern shore,
recruiting all the Spanish men
of Trinidad de Cuba as soldiers,
then seizing all the native Ciboney Taíno men
as enslaved porters for an expedition
of slaughter and conquest, across the western sea
south of Aztlán, land of Moctezuma, ruler of Tenochtitlán.

Only women, children, and singing dogs
were left behind in the village of Trinidad,
along with one guard and one prisoner,
a pacifist called Uría, half Ciboney
and half Canary Islander, a poetic scribe

who loved to write
and refused to fight.

A singing dog led a Ciboney girl called Arima
to the little prison, where she freed Uría,
then helped him escape, and showed him
how to thrive in el monte, wild mountains,
dense jungle, her home.

Now this new boy called Amado is peaceful like Uría,
and the girl named Liana is brave like Arima,
so the modern dog's task is clear —
just guide these two young people until
they accept each other's companionship.
Some matches are simply
meant to be.

If you lived in another time and place,
you might think of the singing dog as a winged thing:
Eros.
Cupid.
A guardian
who specializes
in love.

Admiration
Liana

The tall boy is calm like a palm tree
when standing motionless,
then fiery as a solar flare
as he rages against poverty,
blaming all three governments—
Cuba for failing to plant food crops,
the US for isolating us with a senseless
trade embargo, and Russia for making us so
completely dependent on handouts that when
we're abandoned
we starve.

The boy is smart
honest
gentle.

It's enough to make my heart and mind
feel as wide and far-reaching as the sky.

Confusion Is Another Word for Wishes

Amado

The girl is
eye-light
dream-light
fierce-bright
so perfectly
furiously
intelligent
and yet
she seems
distant
as if she
might
suddenly
flee.

Inventing a Meal

Liana

Why waste energy on daydreams
when I could be foraging?

I tell myself to think of nothing but food
and the dog, whom I decide to call Paz,
because he brings me such an unusual
form of peace, the kind of tranquility
that feels liberating, like a wild
sigh
of relief.

Back at the beach the next evening,
Paz and I conjure a supper of coiled seaweed,
plopping it into the milky heart of a coconut
that I salvaged
from a towering
palm tree.

Just enough food
to make me feel even more
hollow.

Aquatic
Amado

When I see the girl stirring
something mysterious
I'm drawn to a view of green slime,
food suitable only for seagulls.

Inventar. Invent.
Resolver. Solve problems.
No es fácil. It's not easy.
La lucha. The struggle.
Without my brother's
poetic code words,
where would I be?

Determined to invent, resolve, work hard,
and struggle, I plunge into a rocky coral pool,
my eager fist rewarding me with a tightly clasped
moray eel, grabbed right behind the head like a snake,
to make the ferocious teeth
helpless.

Skinned eel flesh, the cracked claws of red crabs,
smelly seaweed,
sweet coconut milk,
all of it boiled and swirled,
then swallowed. . . .

Such a bizarre feast,
spontaneously created
and recklessly shared
with a girl who barely
acknowledges
that I exist.

Why do I fool myself into imagining
a bonfire of warm, explosive passion,
when all she's willing to radiate
is this cold light
of wave-washed
indifference?

The Music of Food

Liana

Paz sings
while I cook with driftwood.

The tall boy joins in, more wolf howl
than melody.

Horizon of waves.
Wind on the beach.
My own voice is silence,
this slowly gathered
secretive
strength.

We eat like ravenous beasts,
slurping
gurgling
murmuring
syllables of gratitude
for a weird meal
of satisfying
scraps.

Attraction
Liana

Embers flare
within the heart's sky
like fireflies that blink
as they search
for mates.

Natural.
Musical.
Rhythmic.

The pulse in my mind wanders away
from hunger, toward something I can barely name.
A spark
of wishlight
on the dark horizon's
oceanic warmth.

If only I could allow my voice to burn energy,
admitting that I truly crave this boy's
smile.

Her Eyes Are . . .
Amado

magnets, a force of gravity pulling me downward,
an ability to draw patterns of movement along
this earth-and-sea surface, like moon tides
or tree roots
sinking.

But love
at first, second, third,
or ten millionth glimpse
is mythical,
isn't
it?

Night Hunger
Amado

I walk home alone,
leaving the girl and her eerie dog
immersed in their private world
of wordless
communication.

Apagón. Blackout.
No power.
No lights.
I won't
be able to read or write.

No way to watch preparations
for the global games
on our old black-and-white
Russian television.

So I go to bed early, dreaming
of a skinny sirena, a mermaid,
musical
ingenious
maybe even
dangerous.

Imaginary
or real?

In dreams
and daydreams
there is no difference.

Maybe love at first sight actually does exist
for those who are well-fed enough
to
sleep.

Wide Awake
Amado

Picturing the girl, I can't keep my eyes closed.
I think of my parents in the other room,
married for decades, affectionate, faithful.
They mourn my decision to defy the authorities,
even though they insist they're supportive
in a skeptical way.

Now I'll never be chosen for a good school,
mamá warns, and I'll always be treated
like a dangerous criminal, papá admonishes,
as if being the brother of a political prisoner
weren't already risky enough.

Fear-stricken.
Fright-sickened.
Petrified by my
damaged future.

If I let myself absorb that parental terror
I'll fade away like a meteor, all my natural fire
destroyed.

Priorities
Liana

Amado is a word that means loved.
Who would give an ordinary boy
such an old-fashioned name?

His mother must be one of those romantic women
who lacks a modern imagination, she probably
embroiders or makes lace in her spare time,
following traditions left over from long ago.

If Amado thinks I'll fall for him, he's wrong.
He's attractive in his own howling way
but I don't need a boyfriend—not now
during this food crisis, when all I crave
should be calories,
although somehow
I seem to be swallowing
more fantasies of romance than actual food.

If only Amado
were not so appealing. . . .

Perseverance
The singing dog

Nose-reach. It's the length of a dog's ability to sniff,
a canine measure of inhaled distance.

The only thing he understands is how to lead, guide,
breathe, so he persists, following any scent that smells
delicious, because without aromas, there can be
no flavors. Taste has an odor, and every mouth
needs to savor the air that surrounds
each
fragrant
bite.

His quest for food continues,
along with the true goal: togetherness.
Love.

Daybreak

Liana

Waves, sky, birds,
all this natural expanse of beauty
does not seem to belong to the same world
    as starvation.

Each gust of wind
makes me think of breakfast
while Paz and I scan soft sand in search
of a freshly beached flying fish.
Sometimes they leap so far that they land
in this terrestrial realm, where empty air
is the only abundant
          substitute
             for fullness.

Breathe, listen, gaze, reach—I imitate
every one of the dog's optimistic actions
as he leads me toward
sunlit
             possibilities.

Pessimism
Amado

How unnatural the dog's eagerness seems.
Can't he see that we're spending too much energy
in our constant effort to gain scraps of nutrition?

Selfish, greedy, suspicious,
narrow,
that's how I feel,
just as thin
and threadlike
as a strand
of seaweed,
that can vanish
without being noticed
by the tide.

Jokes and riddles
used to keep my brother cheerful.
What are the three successes of the revolution?
Sports, medicine, literacy.
What are the three failures?
Breakfast, lunch, dinner.

By the time he went to prison
we were already so close to starving
that his humor grew increasingly grim.

What do all young cubanos want to be
when we grow up
he would ask,
providing the cynical answer
himself:
Extranjeros.
Foreigners.

Too Many Mirrors
Liana

Each time I glimpse my form
in a watery reflection
or a window,
I see clothing so shabby
that I resemble a witch in a fairy tale.

What the mirrors don't show
is even worse, hidden beneath
ragged shirts and faded shorts:
underwear
in shreds,
the soft cloth
falling apart
in so many places
that it shifts like clouds
on a sky
of bronze flesh.

There is no way to feel comfortable, dressed
in this restless cotton storm—but finding
new clothes
would be just as impossible
as trying to buy

beef
or optimism.

All I can do
is search the beach,
hoping to locate a few wisps
of floating fabric that can be cut and stitched
to create an illusion of garments.

Each time I go home to my worried parents
I stare into their starving eyes
and feel
guilty.

Under ordinary circumstances, they would never
allow me to ramble unsupervised
like a ghost.

When I talk to them, they answer, but never
honestly, because they want to reassure me
in a situation so desperate that the truth
would be cruel.

A Cautious Conversation
Liana

Mami asks what I do when I'm gone
for hours on end, so I pretend
that I run on the beach,
training so I can try out
for a school team
that might lead
to the Olympics
or some other
games.

Imagínate, I say, hoping she'll obey
and imagine me winning races
in some future version of this year's
Juegos panamericanos,
so that I can be successful
even without being accepted
to medical school . . .

but we both know the government
won't choose me for any athletic program either,
not after I rejected my chance to demonstrate
absolute, unquestioning
patriotic loyalty.

Imagínate, Mami echoes,
just imagine how terrible it would be
to live someplace else, in another country
with fewer opportunities!

She shouts it loudly, bellowing
to make sure neighbors overhear her
if they happen to be passing by on the street
and cup one ear against our wall, trying
to determine whether I'm really
as notoriously lazy
or dangerously
traitorous
as the local gossips
will surely
insist.

Secret Police
Amado

State Security agents stroll along our street
even more often than they check up
on real criminals.

Any home where one teenager has refused
to show up for military service, and another evades
summer labor
is a place where other forbidden ideas
might be discovered,
so the plainclothesmen
in their dark slacks,
white guayabera shirts,
and polished black leather shoes
watch, watch, watch our house
to see who comes in
or goes out.

Each time I leave to meet Liana, I flee
through a back door, never the visible front.
I leave my parents vulnerable, but life has already
turned into nothing but an endless list of dangers.

Neighborhood Spies
Amado

El Comité is even worse,
a committee for defense of the revolution
that consists of old women who pretend
to visit, then ask to use the bathroom
just so they can peek
to see
if we
read
banned
foreign
magazines
or if we use official
government newsletters
disrespectfully
as toilet paper.

Grandparents
Amado

To escape from the gloom
of my own home, I visit my abuelos
in the next town, only thirty kilometers away
but with so few buses running
that I have to hitchhike, riding in a neighbor's
horse-drawn wagon
that doubles as an ambulance
whenever people who have cars
can't find fuel.

What a shock it is to discover
that my rugged, cigar-smoking grandma
is almost blind
from malnutrition.

Instead of a Seeing Eye dog,
she depends on a guide pony
with a sweet expression and shaggy black mane.

Indoors, the little pony seems enormous,
even though outside it would be no more
noticeable than the average goat.

The first hour of my visit is wasted
on wishing for protein, vitamins, and courage

for Abuela, who has always been terrified
of dogs, simply because when she was little
a pack of strays
chased her.

Now, she reminisces about her childhood
when she plowed with a team of oxen,
raised hogs, milked cows, and sprinkled
broken corn kernels on the ground each morning
to keep a dozen hens happy.

Eggs.
Butter.
Meat.
Fresh vegetables.
She names all the foods she believes
she needs, to restore her eyesight.

Abuelo sends me out to neglected
government fields, where I use a machete
to steal fibrous stalks of weedy grasses,
piling green fodder onto my shoulders,
then hauling it back to the house
as a gift for the little pony

that leads Abuela
down the cobblestone street
to a ration outlet, where shelves
are so bare
that all we can buy
is syrupy cane,
the same sugar
that grows in fields
all around us
every day.

Azúcar, my grandfather says with a sigh,
remembering sweeter times
and balanced diets.

Mercifully, he lives on a menu of memories,
while my generation needs to survive
on nothing
but wishes.

The Distance of Relatives
Liana

When Amado tells me about his abuelos
I wonder about my own, all four gone
long before I was born.

They lived on small subsistence farms
until the revolution forced them to collectivize,
sharing family land with strangers, a sacrifice
that destroyed their will to plow, plant, fertilize,
harvest,
thrive.

Now all I have are primos, tíos, and padrinos, a wealth
of loving relations who rarely visit, simply because
we all know we can't offer even the smallest
morsel of food
to any guest.

The next time Amado goes to see his grandparents
I'll ask him to take me with him, so I can learn
the skills of old folks—agriculture, and how
to raise chickens. . . .

I'll have to leave Paz at home,
so he doesn't terrify Amado's abuela.

How strange it is to think of humanity's
variety of fears.

My own worst terror is starving, dying young,
right now, this year, long before I have a chance
to grow up and fall
spinning
twirling
plummeting
down
down
down
into
the dizzy
heights
of love.

Tyranny
Liana

Hunger
is a bully
who punishes me
for imagining comfort,
each bite of hollow wishes
bringing more belly pain,
not less.

So I chew a solid mass of roadside weeds
just to show the tyrant a glimpse of defeat.

After vomiting and diarrhea
I give up.

Tyranny triumphs.
I am a prisoner
of emptiness.

Strategy
Amado

Hunger is a weapon of war.
El período especial en tiempos de paz
means the suffering of warfare without bullets
or blades.

We need a defensive plan.
My cautious parents insist on waiting.
My nostalgic grandparents gaze back at memories.
The government expects obedient patience.
Liana and her wild dog believe in foraging
like roaming nomads from a long-lost wilderness,
but I long for a geographic solution to island problems.

Fly?
Swim?
Run?
Race?
No, there's no way to reach any distant shore
so I end up with no plan, just air, breath, survival
from one rhythmic inhalation
to the next.

Nutrients
Liana

I could fill my mind with fantasies of protein,
amino acids, vitamins, minerals, fat.

Or I can switch my brain to an imaginary
television channel where all I see
is eyes
your face
hopes
thoughts
Amado.

Impatience
Amado

I don't know how to wait forever.
We could wander hand in hand
instead of wasting away all summer.

Your distance.
My shyness.
Patience.
Patience.
Patience.
Of course I'll wait to speak
touch
reach
forever.

Summer Street

Liana

Music, drums,
dancing, rum,
arm wrestling,
domino games,
everything festive
happens at night,
outdoors
in dark
moist heat
al aire libre
the free air of rainstorms
and power blackouts
when there's no point pretending
to be cool enough
for sleep.

Parties without food.
Celebrations of survival.
A rebellion against the strength
of hunger.

Solitude
Amado

Night after night, this darkness,
each electrical blackout a reminder
that our lightless village
is invisible
from space.

We are unknown
to the rest
of the universe.

No one is aware
that we're starving.

If they knew,
would they care?

I could join the street dance,
but why not waste away alone
when hunger leaves me listless
loveless
bare.

Scentscape
The singing dog

Just when they're most desperate,
the dog shows them how to join together again,
following wind-whispery trails,
doing aerial and soil-borne nose work
that guides them toward the radiant centers of smells,
helping them enter the essence
of any animal they track, living or lost,
a fish
on the beach,
duck eggs at the edge
of a mangrove swamp,
tree snails climbing
twined branches.

In this folded landscape of layered odors,
the canine nose teaches humans how to shovel
sky and soil, to expose
endurance.

Animal-Joy
Amado

The singing dog helps us locate each other
every morning, so that together we find scraps
to munch, sharing morsels of palm grubs, frog legs,
sea trash. . . .

When quiet Liana finally speaks, we discuss
the greed of all creatures that need to eat.

She says we are hideously selfish and secretive,
we should be struggling to feed our families
along with little kids on the street, old folks,
neighbors, even strangers, and my abuelos . . .

but if the eggness of a duck egg is enough aroma
to yield a meal, then isn't the hunger of humans
just as fragrant in some significant way?
My belly's need makes me dizzy with questions.
All I crave is a restful mind and my hammock,
a nap, because sometimes there is nothing
more exhausting
than fantasies of happiness.

Fear-Breath
Liana

Aromatic trees in an orchard,
the dog's calmness, and Amado's vigilance
as we steal orange mangos that smell like dreams.

If we're caught, we could be sent away
for much longer than a summer
of forced labor.

You never know if you're a criminal
until your hollow belly cramps
with the pain
of exhilarating
lawlessness.

Fishing Song
Amado

At least once each day I make up some excuse
to fool my parents into imagining that I'm behaving
like a responsible son, searching for food to share
with them.

At least once each day, Liana and I dive,
trying to catch anything digestible,
a threshold that changes, depending
on the intensity of our shared
hunger.

Fish often escape, leaving us with nothing but
unidentifiable creatures that look leafy, and plants
that seem to be prehistoric animals.

Not knowing which organisms are toxic
we often end up filled with regrets instead of protein.

So we fashion hooks from wire and stand holding rods
that are just branches, as we continue to hope
that patience will be enough
to fool a fish into believing illusions
created by floating lures made of feathers.

Long Before the Games Begin
Amado

It happens to be a day of electricity,
so everyone all over town can watch
foreign athletes who arrive in the city early,
hoping to grow accustomed
to our hot, humid climate.

Televised cheers
blast from hundreds
of wide-open windows
as every neighbor shares
the excitement.

For one brief moment, I experience
a sense of unity with remote nations
all over the world.

How odd it is that throwing, catching,
or kicking a ball is enough to make people feel like
we're capable of understanding one another's
distance.

Imagining Secrecy
Liana

I watch the sports frenzy,
listen to neighbors' drums,
join another street dance,
and pay attention to people
who seem unnaturally
energetic.

Where do they find enough food
for such enthusiastic celebrations?

La bolsa negra.
The black bag.
There's no other clear explanation.
They must know illegal marketeers
who steal food, then secretly sell it.

What will I find if I follow like a shadow?
Sweet potatoes? Cabbage?
Cashews? Chicken?

My Most Secretive Secret
Amado

I imagine meals
and kisses
the echo
of hunger
more hungers.

If Only
Liana

With no money and no surplus to trade
on the black market, we need to keep
scrounging just enough for ourselves
or learn to live
like our ancestors,
planting, harvesting,
hunting,
gathering. . . .

We need to visit
Amado's abuelos.

In Heaven There Will Be Vegetables

Amado

We're greeted with food!
Abuelo has planted a garden
hidden at the heart of their house,
in the small central courtyard,
el patio where my grandma keeps
her little pony
so close
that he never
      has a chance to devour
  the yellow yams
    and green beans
       spreading out
in all directions,
    like scouts
from a bee hive,
      searching
for delicious
nectar.

En el cielo, my grandpa assures me
there will be vegetables.

Mentors
Liana

This is exactly what we need,
agricultural wisdom that ends
with something we can actually eat,
not just the usual sweet, fibrous cane
grown by forcing bitter teenagers
to volunteer on sugar farms.

Why didn't the government ever diversify,
planting a variety of food crops?

Soil, water, silence—
the old folks' garden
yields more than words
can communicate.

We follow their example,
move when they move,
wrap tomato stems
around wooden stakes
to make the plants obey
our suggestions
as we guide them, green
and hopeful

upward
toward sunlight.

Imagine
how much nutrition
this whole island would enjoy
if every young person learned
from old farmers!

You-Know-Who
Amado

Halter and lead line,
we go out exploring,
to help the pony locate
wild grasses to munch.

As we stroll, I become aware
of our unspoken conversation.

We never mention the bearded man
who makes every decision about farming,
although he has no agronomic training at all.

We never speak of the endlessly televised speeches
where he tries to make failure sound like success
as he brags about fields and livestock
that don't exist, ignoring the advice
of scientists, economists, historians. . . .

We don't dare to discuss the lies
he portrays as truth, because even
the use of sign language
to draw an imaginary beard
in the air
is dangerous enough to get us

arrested
on suspicion of criticizing
the dictator
we refer to as
tú-sabes-quién.

Power Is Fattening
Liana

There must be calories
in you-know-who's long, boring speeches,
because while the rest of us grow
more and more skeletal,
the bearded man
remains chubby.

He's already ruled Cuba
for more than thirty years.
Why doesn't he give someone
younger
and less selfish
a chance?

Journey
Amado

The road home is slow and quiet,
each of us lost
in the memory
of so much advice
from my abuelos:
Eat everything on your plate.
Experiment, don't be afraid to take chances.
Break the law if obeying it will condemn you
to starvation.

Never lose hope,
but don't wait for other countries
to save us either, because look how long the US
trade embargo has persisted: nearly thirty years,
three decades of hatred adding to the depth
of our homegrown hunger, and see how easily
Russia abandoned us, after promising
to support Cuba's economy
forever.

Hunters

Liana and Amado

That night, there are only two flimsy wings
but we share, chewing slowly
enjoying the silence
of wordless
gulps.

Bones,
flesh, and skin
from a roasted pigeon
seem magical, as if mere shapes
can give our minds strength to fly.

When you've already lost a fourth
of your body weight, eating a wild bird
cooked over a campfire in a park at midnight
feels normal, even when you're sneaking
out at night like a burglar, defying parental rules
and stealing from nature.
We feed the liver and gizzard to Paz,
knowing he won't mind strong flavors
and powerful smells.

Two Verbs for Knowledge
Liana and Amado

Lips meet. Wishes twist. Hunger and fear
are no longer our only obsessions.

Until our first kiss,
conocer was all we possessed, just that casual
acquaintance, a faint recognition of the shape
and nature
of mouths.

Saber.
To know.
Now we truly understand
the simultaneous simplicity and complexity
of curiosity
and other
ravenous
mysteries.

The World Suddenly Begins to Spin More Swiftly!

Liana

I'm still young, but now
I've kissed and been kissed,
I'm still hungry, but
food is no longer
my only wish.

A Home on the Roof
Amado

Once I've traveled to the universe
of kisses, nothing else really matters.

I sweep water off the roof tiles of our house
after a rainstorm, then stretch out and gaze up
at heaven, intensely aware that heaven, el cielo,
is also close, not just remote.

Hope is here, all over this starving isle,
mixed up with the tragic hunger that forces
gentle people to slaughter pigeons
in parks,
plucking feathers,
roasting, swallowing,
then kissing
between gulps
of starlight.

Success

The singing dog

Matchmaking is as mysterious as the sonar
that emanates from bats in a seaside cave's
darkness.

It's enough to know that Liana and Amado
belong
together.

Understanding is not needed,
only closeness.

Shape-Shifting
Amado and Liana

Slowly at first
then swiftly
we emerge
from our childhood selves
renewed as two nearly grown creatures
who have learned to speak courageously,
abandoning shy silence
in order to accept
         wonder.

Now we are almost as attracted
to each other's words and thoughts
as to hands, bodies, eyes, smiles, lips,
sight   sound   taste   scent
touch.

Love in a Time of Wonder

Liana and Amado and the singing dog

Hunger
or love?

Hunger
   before
      love.

Love   beyond   hunger
hunger   love   hunger
love   hunger   love
love.

Ode to Paz

Amado and Liana

Roaming
nomad
unpredictable
visitor
exhaling
aromas
of
love's
hunger
and
hunger's
love.

Garden Song
Amado and Liana

Once again we visit the old folks, who grant us a gift
of pumpkin seeds, and the promise of avocados
from a potted tree, the slender trunk wrapped
in copper bracelets just in case old legends
are true, about the magical properties of shiny
red metal, said to combat plant diseases,
or turn into a poison
if too much is received.

Paz is with us this time, Abuela and her pony
both too happy to cling to childhood fears of feral dogs.

The garden is lush and bountiful
like a dream-forest, overflowing with marvels.
Roots.
Leaves.
Fruit.

Time seems to stop
as soon as we see food growing.
Now it's our job to go home and plant, eat, share.

Love
Amado

Plant, harvest,
right away,
no delay,
it's the only way
to feel hopeful!

Beyond Love
Liana

My parents worry—are we breaking rules?
No one knows exactly how long it has been
since anyone in this family grew
our own food.

Within Love
Amado and Liana

We convince our reluctant parents, then urge them
to help us dig holes and bury seeds, as the reality
of unimagined possibilities
begins
to take
root!

Our Parents Warn Us That We're Taking Chances

Liana and Amado

Being independent.
Making our own decisions.
Risking trouble in exchange
for producing anything that exceeds
monthly rations.

What if we're suspected of planting crops
in order to sell food on the black market?

Our Answer
Amado and Liana

We're hungry.
Earth helps us.
Let's grow.

The Names of Love 1
Liana

Cielo tierra hoja mar sol
luna estrella esperanza.

The Names of Love 2

Amado

She calls me
sky earth leaf sea sun
moon stars hope.

I answer that wherever there is hope there is love
and whenever there is peace we have hope
and eating enough is part of feeling peaceful.

The Names of Love 3
Liana and Amado

Vastness invisible past present future
there's no end to claiming and naming
this limitless
wilderness
of mysteries.
Our lives.

Balseros
Liana

We still sneak out of our houses at night,
despite our parents' warnings, protests,
and futile attempts at punishment.
Nothing they take from us matters,
because we have no luxuries, no privileges,
just hunger
and time.

So we sneak out carrying fireflies in bottles
whenever we can't find batteries for flashlights.
Needing a place to be alone, we're led by Paz.
The seaside cave is a plain one, simple.
No stalactites or crystals, just smooth walls
marked with red, blue, and yellow pictures
of eyes, wings,
hands, hearts.

We're not alone here.
Inner tubes.
Ropes.
Rough brown gourds
filled with fresh water.
Dried guavas, stale bread,
and peeled spears of sugar cane.

Two people, a young man
and his heavily pregnant wife
are clearly terrified by our presence
as they try to hide in a dark corner,
unable to evade our captive insects'
pulsing light.

Leaving the island is forbidden by law
and it's equally illegal
to know that someone is planning to flee.

We're required
to report escapees
to the authorities
but how can we
betray strangers
who are simply
hoping
to avoid
the same
plague of hunger
that has tormented us
for so long?

Anyone who takes the time to paint
murals of primary colors on cave walls
deserves a chance to float freely
los balseros
the rafters
fleeing refugees
buoyed by hope.

Throwing Oneself Into the Sea
Amado

Before he chose prison, my brother considered
the possibility of building a raft and soaring away
on a flimsy contraption made from inner tubes
and rope . . .

but the chances of surviving are unknown, perhaps
fifty-fifty
or less.

No one can count the tens of thousands of bodies
already lost halfway between here and the other side
of the Florida Straits—Key West, Miami,
the United States of Plenty.

If I had enough hoarded food to make it safely across
days or weeks on waves, surrounded by sharks,
would I nibble slowly, or swallow it all
right now
here in this cavern,
like a prehistoric beast?

Compass
Liana

We leave the cave quickly,
reassuring the frightened couple
that their secret is safe.

The next morning at home
I search my imagination for any gift
that might help them, something I can find
or make, before it's too late.

Of all the supplies a balsero would need,
una brújula seems the most basic,
an old-fashioned compass, magical like witchery,
yet scientific too,
one of the projects small children learn
by reading old adventure books.

Take a needle from your mother's sewing kit
and an iron nail from your father's toolbox,
rub the needle against the nail fifty times,
every stroke in the same direction, never
back and forth, then: metal on metal,
a magnetic charge is created.
If you can't find a nail, use your own hair,
or even mouse fur.

Pierce a cork or a juicy green leaf
from a sea grape tree, and let the magnetized gadget
twirl in a shallow bowl of water, watch it spin
and settle,
selecting
north.

How long will this fragment of ancient technology
last?

We take it back to the cave.
We don't ask for any form of payment.
Instead, we help fill two slick black inner tubes
with breath, then tie them together—coiled hope
    goodbye
        please
            float . . .

Departure
The singing dog

Human desperation smells like a marsh, sour
and fermented, but the dog knows how
to cheer people by keeping them moving
toward a goal, the next scent
a promising one—home, kitchen, nutrition,
the imagination's ability to conjure a fragrance
of daydreamed
arrival.

Cause and Effect
Liana

Loving each other.
Helping others.
It's a combination
we never imagined
when all we felt
was physical
attraction.
Separate bellies.
Wondering minds.
Shared hearts.

Black Market
Amado

We need more seeds for our gardens,
a greater variety of edible promises.

There's only one way.
We'll have to plunge ourselves
into la bolsa negra,
the shadowy, nomadic network
of illegal marketeers
where secretive people
sell, bargain, and trade
as if profits were not forbidden.

We discover places where we could ask
for stolen government supplies:
kernels of seed corn,
malanga tubers, grapefruit seedlings, and peanuts
that we desperately wish we could swallow
instead of planting.

We have nothing to trade, no antiques, jewelry
or other treasures left over from long ago,
so we're limited to exchanging things we find
on the beach.

Plastic sandals.
Broken toys.
Empty soda cans.

More and more often
we find discarded possessions
in the cave—boots, photo frames,
a cradle, baseballs, two paintings,
all sorts of objects heavy enough
to make any overcrowded raft
                    sink.

So we carry these secrets
in an old cloth sack
as if they were smuggled
from overseas.

In black market alleys
it will be easy—but dangerous—to trade them
for garden dreams, our deeply rooted
future.

Gardens of Dreaming
Liana and Amado and the singing dog

Every available
centimeter of soil
in both patios
is soon covered
with a dozen
variations
      of green,
the leafiness
as hopeful
as a steamy
afternoon's
soothing
      breeze.

Above the Soil
Liana

Our fingers touch as we work,
lips meet, each quiet kiss
a wishful
forest
of growth.

Our parents decide to pretend
they don't see.
If we succeed, they'll have plenty
to eat.

If neighbors or secret policemen notice
that we've been haunting the black market,
we'll bribe them with green leaves
and crispness—cabbage in exchange
for silence, cucumbers to ward off
danger, red peppers to spice
the risk.

Readers and Singers
Amado

While we wait for food to spring upward
from the hidden wizardry of buried earth,
we scheme and wonder, trying to figure out
what to eat in the meantime, and how to help
more and more balseros
obtain supplies they'll need
for survival
at sea.

Liana's parents are lectores at a cigar factory,
taking turns reading to workers who sit in rows,
cutting and rolling pungent tobacco leaves.

Each month, laborers vote, choosing books
for the next few weeks of drudgery.

Novels, poetry, plays, whatever they read,
the voices of Liana's mother and father
entrance me each time we visit and listen,
pretending we're interested in obtaining jobs,
although really all we're doing is spying,
hoping to discover a box or bin
that might contain discarded cigars

of an inferior quality, trash we could silently
scoop up and trade on la bolsa negra
without getting caught
and arrested for theft.

Stealing from a government building
is not as easy as it seemed when we
were just daydreaming.

A soldier stands at the exit, humming along
while Liana's mother bursts into song,
expanding her role from reader to singer,
the lyrics a passionate ballad
of love.

Surrounded by Music

Liana

I grew up hearing Mami sing every day,
so it never occurred to me that someone else
might be surprised by the fountain of music
that flows all around me
like sun
at the end of a storm,
warmth and light interwoven
to form melodies.

We leave the cigar factory without any treasure
to trade or sell, just a new, radiant memory
that did not exist until now, my mother's voice
rising above silence, her personal protest
against pessimism.

No one who hears
a beautiful love song
can fail to imagine
life beyond hunger.

Harvest
The singing dog

The houses of both humans are now frames
for hidden roots that lift hope toward sky.

There is an aroma of movement
as folded seed-leaves open
and the tips of stems
reach like fingers.

That first red radish makes the girl and boy
celebrate by dancing along with their parents,
but the dog waits for sweet potatoes and melons,
plump foods that help the world smell sunlit.

When he started this matchmaking project
he had no idea that love between two teenagers
would lead to so much shared
human and canine
rejoicing!

A Vision of Independence
Amado and Liana

In the time of our grandparents' youth,
everyone knew how to care for oxen and horses,
how to plow, plant, cultivate, and harvest,
but my parents' generation was forced to wait
for beans and rice to reach the ration store,
imported from Vietnam or China.

Our mothers sifted small grains
like rough jewels, picking through them
to discard insects, weed seeds, and pebbles.

It's a ritual we've seen so often, without wondering
why we don't grow our own arroz y frijoles, but now
everything has changed inside our minds
so that we are intensely aware of our ability
to seize control of hunger,
transforming food
into freedom.

Creativity
Liana

At night
in the cave
we are witnesses
to the hasty construction of rafts
made from sugar carts, bus roofs,
windshields, couch cushions, mattresses. . . .

Almost any object will float
when fastened to huge inner tubes
from truck tires, as long as the tubes are filled
with air, the sky's breath
generously shared.

How easy it seems to grow
beyond
limits.

Ignorance
Amado

We carve the stored sunlight
of a stolen pineapple
into brilliant puzzle pieces,
trying to figure out
which gold or green part
to bury in soil.

Is it like a potato that can sprout from
fragments, or are we free to gobble
all these juices, reserving only stiff leaves
for experimentation?

If only we had a whole plant
with growing roots and stems.

If only my farm-smart abuelos
lived closer.

Tourist
Liana

A surfer.
Young.
Alone.
He's the first foreigner either of us
has ever seen, with the exception
of Russian soldiers.

Canadian?
British?
Dutch?
We'll never know, because he plunges
into the ocean, paddles out on his board,
and spends the whole morning
waiting
for waves.

If speaking to foreigners were legal,
we could guide him toward more tumultuous waters
just a few hundred meters away from this calmness.

A Farfetched Fantasy
Liana

Sooner or later, the surfer will grow tired.
What can he eat, in this town with no hotels
or restaurants, no taxis either, just horses
and old cars that look like broken clocks
under the hood, an assortment of stray wires,
gears, and coiled springs all held together
with cardboard
and duct tape.

How did the foreigner reach us?
Are there black market taxis now,
or is the government starting
to change those old rules?

I think about our lives
as I try to see myself
through the eyes
of a traveler.

Mothers, children, old folks, and fishermen
have all gathered around, watching, wondering,
waiting to find out
what the surfer will do.

The enigma seems so simple.
All he does is ride small, lazy waves,
balancing in a way that reminds me
of our daily struggle to juggle reality
and wishes, always ending up creating
a makeshift assortment of fantasies.

Maybe he has learned to be
just as inventive as we are.
If I offer him a creative snack
will he accept, would he pay?

How much might a tourist give
for two handfuls of roasted peanuts?

Would a marketeer accept foreign money
as payment for our purchases, and could we
manage all these transactions without
being caught?

The Comfort of Nature
Amado

I imagine this beach
as seen through the eyes of the surfer.

Infinite sun, sugar-fine sand, all the colors
and crystalline light of a coral reef
where rainbow-hued creatures
drift
and dart
like dreams.

If only hunger
never clouded my vision.

I would treasure the sight of natural beauty
every day, instead of hunting for sea beings
to gobble.

Ideas, Part 1
Amado

Imagine
balancing
on a board
that resembles
an enormous fish
while sharks
lurk below
and the sun
flares
above.

The surfer moves
like a rafter,
trusting
this stubborn sea.

Could I ever
be brave enough
to rise up
and glide
from one nation
all the way to another?

I think of all the inventions
I've seen, motorcycles made from bicycles
simply by adding parts from old Russian
washing machines,
lamps fashioned from
toothpaste tubes,
bottle caps converted
into dolls and toy trucks,
shards of old vinyl records
combined with telephone components
to create fans for cooling houses,
as if music can be transformed
into a natural
breeze.

Why not use a surfboard to cross
between Cuba and Miami?

It would be no more challenging
than creating stews from seaweed.

Ideas, Part 2
Liana

When Amado speaks of ingenious contraptions,
their images spin around in my mind until I conceive
of my own best invention—a secret restaurant,
hidden
perilously
inside
my home,
right beside
the garden!

With just a few tables in our courtyard,
I could feed any foreign sports fans
who manage to make their way
from the global games
to our town, our beach. . . .

All I'd have to do is wait
until they look thirsty,
then hungry, ravenous,
desperate,
just like us.

Ideas, Part 3
Amado

Enriqueciendo is the most serious crime.
Getting rich by selling is far more risky
than buying on the black market.

Liana's punishment for creating a secret restaurant
would be drastic.
Even this chatter about the possibility of a business
intended for profit
could get us arrested if we're overheard
by informers.

No, I tell her, don't do it, let's not even try.
When I go to prison, let it be for pacifism,
not greed. . . .

A Restaurant for Survival
Liana

It wouldn't be greed, I argue vehemently,
not if all I do is cook enough and sell enough
to keep myself and my family alive.

Amado and I storm off in different directions,
forcing Paz to choose between us, a dilemma
so frustrating that the poor dog stands alone
halfway between us, looking lost.

Imagine all the meals I could serve!
Wild rabbit, wild boar, a random assortment
of bait fish, what wouldn't a spoiled foreigner eat
when faced with the reality of hunger?

Spark
Amado

Again
and again
day
after day
we argue
the same way
we kiss,
each syllable
of our dispute
fiery.

We rage
the same way
we embrace,
each atom
of skin
and bone
flaming.

Independence
Liana

I can't let Amado's fear
rule my future.

He's supposed to be my boyfriend,
not my boss.

I'm free
to ignore his opinions.

So what will I call my restaurant?
Sabor, to make sure hungry foreigners
know they can expect flavor . . .

or Palacio de sabor, but it won't be a palace,
just a patio at the heart of an ordinary home.
Better yet, Paladar, a fancy word that honors
the sensitive human palate, a delicate way
of just barely suggesting glorious
flavors
to savor.

Resilience
The singing dog

Crisscrossed pathways of teenage wishes,
a scent of suspicion,
no way to unite two divided individuals,
but the dog is stubborn too,
his goal so clear and fragrant,
nothing more nor less
than love's relentless persistence.
Now that they're arguing,
he needs to remember
time's
aroma.

In 1522, when the conquering Spaniards returned
to Trinidad de Cuba with Aztec captives,
the fugitives Uría and Arima were already safe
in green mountains
with their singing dog
and a laughing baby.

Now, this modern dog knows he must figure out how
to lead Amado and Liana back toward each other.
Impossible? Almost. So he curls up
in the comforting shade

of a sea grape tree on the beach,
inhaling the free flow
of scented canine daydreams
from long ago.

Hunger and Anger Are Synonyms
Amado

As soon as I storm off on my own, I know
that I won't eat all day, not without Liana
to calm
these spikes
of rage
that gnaw
at my belly
from inside
like sharp teeth
as if I'm being
consumed
by fangs
of air.

Together, we always find food and hope,
but alone
all I have
is stark
fury.

The Stench of Confusion

Liana

Paz finds me the next morning
by following my odor of turmoil.

He gazes quietly, as if he understands
that I'm forcing myself to focus,
concentrate, stay busy, plan, scheme. . . .

It takes an effort to forget about Amado,
shoving our argument about an illegal restaurant
out of my thoughts, like a villain in a half-waking
nightmare.

Questioned
Amado

I've been cautious for years, all my opinions
about military service strictly private, never public,
so when two well-fed men with clean clothes
and polished shoes
take me aside and ask to see
my identification card and ration book,
my heart flies up to my throat
like a zoo-creature
struggling
to escape
from its tiny
cage.

The questions are simple.
They sound like statements.
How is my brother, did I know
that he's organized a hunger strike in prison.
How can anyone choose to eat less at a time
like this, instead of more, am I a fanatic
like him, have I answered any messages
delivered by a smuggler, don't I know he'll die
if he continues refusing to eat worm-ravaged
prison rations, won't he be known as a fool

instead of a martyr, maybe you're different,
perhaps you like reality better than fantasies,
don't you.

I have no answers.
No guesses.
No voice.

Just my head, nodding automatically
like a robot, as I promise to be practical
and realistic
instead of idealistic.

My Silent Answers
Amado

Hermano, your stomach must be so empty,
muscles and bone quietly disintegrating,
mind dancing in slow-motion circles,
weak arms wrapped around memory's
shadow.

Small Gestures
Amado

Every time I'm followed by those two
investigators, I stray far enough away
from Liana and Paz
to keep them safely out of view.

Even if she decides to start some crazy
profitable business that will get her sent away
to a forced labor camp or women's prison,
I have to try to protect her as much as I can,
because love does not care about
wisdom.

Is It True That Foreigners Are Accustomed to Choices?

Liana

I need a menu,
but how many languages,
and is it wise to offer
more than one selection,
and what about the paper shortage,
I'll have to write on blank scraps
torn from old books,
flyleaves
where I'll scribble
three sections:
Sky, Earth, Sea,
with pictures of a dove, cow, and lobster,
even though in real life
I might have to cook
gulls, rats, and scavenged crabs,
half-rotted on the beach.

Why am I doing this,
the eyes and voice
of the singing dog
seem to say.

My only answer is independence.
I need to find out whether it's possible
to live courageously in a time of danger.

Loneliness Forces Me
to Keep Exploring
Liana

While I'm angry with Amado
I grow bolder,
not
more
timid.

Solitude lures me back to the cave at night
to see if any balseros have abandoned
something useful, but instead of the usual
assortment of oddities left behind
by frightened families,
I discover
an entire circus
complete with ruffled costumes.

Fire eater, magician, acrobat, unicyclist,
and tightrope walker, all performing for each other
one last dazzling time before converting
their mended tent into an immense sail
that will whoosh an enormous raft
over horrifying waves
and terrifying wind.

The magician releases white doves,
setting them free instead of sacrificing their flesh
to a saint, as so many travelers would do—
or taking them to sea in cages, to be eaten
in a moment of desperation.

What will I accomplish with this unicycle,
my only payment for a homemade compass
and the promise
of secrecy?

Maybe I can learn to ride it,
then set off across the universe
of galaxies, like an astronaut in a fantasy.

Downpour
Amado

I witness the departure of the circus
after I follow Liana to make sure she's safe.

My vow to stay away from her is impossible to keep.
By crouching in a dark corner of the cavern, I remain
hidden, as I watch and wonder if this is really actual love
or just the pounding of rain, a warm summer torrent
beyond the cave's entrance, a cloudburst
of lightning and thunder,
proof that dark clouds
have bright voices.

My own throat is silent.
The only thing I want to say to Liana
is why take such a risk, please be careful,
no amount of food in your belly is worthy
of a cell so horrific that prisoners
can only escape
by starving.

Generosity Means Restraint
Liana

An arched fan of bananas with sun-yellow peels
and moon-hued interiors, softness, sweetness,
stolen
treasured.

A marketeer accepts the unicycle
in exchange for two legs and the snout
of an illegal pig that was raised in a bathtub,
hidden from neighbors by playing loud music
and letting trash rot, to disguise the squeals
and smell.

Pork!
I could serve it, even though
I imagine most foreigners won't want
to eat the nose if they can see nostrils,
so while my parents are at work, I marinate,
slice, and roast the meat in bartered garlic
and the juice of stolen oranges, a recipe
for fragrance
that I'll have to hide
from passing spies
by filling the kitchen with flowers

and wild herbs, claiming—if anyone asks—
that I'm studying green medicine, the power
of plants
to heal
in this tragic time
of shortages so severe
that even aspirin is just a fading memory.

Doors and windows closed.
Heat, humidity, steam, the smell of meat!
While Paz and I inhale the fierce aroma of protein
I remember how it feels to survive on nothing
but scented air.

When the meal is finally ready, Paz and I gobble
a few precious fragments, saving the rest for my parents
and Amado, maybe even his parents too, and yes,
definitely, soon I'll try to deliver some food
to his abuelos.

For such a generous gift to be possible
I'll have to control my own appetite
and my anger.

A Language of Air
The singing dog

Each human who joins our feast falls silent
under the spell of tormented amazement.

Eating one's fill is a form of guilty magic
when the world all around you is starving.

The singing dog rolls onto his side
and instead of chanting
one of his ancient melodies
he simply breathes un suspiro,
a sigh.

One Question after Another
Amado

Making up after our ugly argument
feels like peaceful sleep after a terrifying dream.

But will we be able to trust each other again?
What if every disagreement leads to separation?
Are we strong enough to accept each other's need
to think and speak
independently?

All I know
is that holding hands
means more to me right now
than clinging desperately
to my own
opinions.

Strange Sights in the Countryside
Liana

On the way to bring meat to Amado's abuelos
we see so many foreigners that we know
the international games must be ready
to spill beyónd Havana, bringing sports
of every sort
to the countryside.
Runners, bicyclists,
even birdwatchers
with binoculars!

The tourists seem to arrive as if by sorcery,
carried in old cars that are suddenly
being used as taxis, or hitchhiking,
expecting mercy just because
the sun is hot
and the wait
is long.

Delay
Liana and Amado

The old folks convince us
to keep any food we grow
for ourselves
and our families.

No restaurant.
No fantasies.

Not now.
Maybe soon,
after the presence of outsiders
forces our government
to change.

Souvenirs for the Future
Liana

Instead of trying to sell food to tourists
I watch them, study their fascination
with flotsam and jetsam
on beaches,
and then I begin to create objects
that will keep forever
so that whenever the laws
are altered
I'll be ready
with sea glass jewelry
to remind travelers
of glittering sand,
and driftwood carved into dolls
decorated with shells, coral, pebbles,
all sorts of gifts from nature
turned into curiosities
for people so wealthy
that all they want to collect
is pleasant memories.

The Gardener's Heart
Amado

Paz has taught me
that memory is a library
of scents and flavors, while fear
is a warehouse of hungers,
so I try to show an interest
in Liana's whimsical effort to imagine
a future of creative opportunities,
but all I really trust
is my own two hands
in deep soil
pulling weeds
and feeding roots
with a shower
of generous
sweat.

Separate Hands
Liana

He gardens.
I make hidden treasures.
Together, we experiment
with independence.

A Message from Prison
Amado

Feeling stranded
even though I'm on shore,
I finally discover a smuggled note
from my brother, just as the secret agents
hinted.

The scrap of paper is on my bed.
Have those policemen entered our house?
I can't ask my parents, because what if
they will be safer not knowing anything
about Generoso. . . .

My brother's name is even more archaic
than mine, as if our wistful mother believed
that she could make the future gentle
by ignoring
harsh centuries.

Stay or leave, Generoso's note advises.
Stay or leave, but don't come
HERE.

Shocked by the recognition of his handwriting,
it's easy for me to see that HERE must mean prison.

All I can glean of his meaning is permission to abandon
our pact, forsake pacifism, stay home and join the military
like I'm supposed to, or flee to some other land
where violence
is voluntary.

Florida is where most rafters end up,
but there's no nation more warlike
than the United States.

Seeing such a cryptic message
makes me feel submerged,
as if I've already fallen off a boat
and I'm drifting
downward,
drowning.

Full Belly, Anxious Mind

Liana

When all the pork is gone
Amado gives me a tomato
as red and ripe as a sunrise,
sliced and shared.

With the global games about to begin
and our gardens growing, and my ideas
flowing, I still feel uncertain, even when my hand
strokes Amado's familiar fingers.

How can love
be enough
in a time
of hunger?

I'm full now, but by tomorrow, once again
we'll be scrounging.

Dilemma
Amado

Stay home or go?
Remain and let the army change my nature
or float away on a raft to some other country
where I'll always
be a stranger?

Such a decision can't be made alone.
First I need to know if Liana
and love
and Paz
will go
with me.

Never
The singing dog

Sometimes the dog understands
human questions.
Is he willing to flee across the sea?

His answer is a howl, not a song,
no rhythm, rhyme, or melody,
just the anguish of centuries suffered.

Stay, humans, stay and share
the mystery of a future
that can only be imagined,
guided, and persuaded,
never
completely
controlled.

Building Hope
Amado

It's silly to ask a dog questions, he doesn't
understand me, and he can't answer, so I begin
to gather bits of wood and string that might
be useful when I construct
our raft.

Is Growth Always So Slow?
Liana

When the games are finally about to begin,
my brothers and all our school friends
return from el campo, wiry and muscular
with sun-roasted skin
and ravenous eyes.

How different life would be if we could all
just roll across the soil like clouds, moving
the way oxen do, ponderously, with gentle gazes
as deep
and dark
as friendship.

Instead, here I am, with a garden that is still
mostly daydreams, waiting for edible
reality.

Ode to Soup
Amado

My mother waited all day in a ration line
until she finally received enough black beans
for sopa, the dark liquid thick and salty, brimming
with green onions that I planted and harvested,
the act of gardening so rewarding
that I feel comforted
from within, as if grains of soil
gathered beneath my fingernails
have a will, choosing
to soothe me.

Rootlets of thought
swirl like soup.
Hot.
Thick.
Nourishing.
It's the closest I've felt to my family
in a long time, the simple act of sharing food
a natural way to remember
relationships.

Overwhelmed
Liana

Truth strikes abruptly.
My brothers are twins, both sixteen.
Soon they'll have to join the army or refuse
and be punished, just like Amado's brother.
Soon Amado will have to make
the same terrible choice.

I've been pushing the thought away
for months, but now it sweeps across me
like a tsunami.

The future seems so twisted,
in their place, I would be furious.

What if they—and Amado—all go to prison,
will I even be permitted
to visit?

The Stadium of Starvation
Amado

Opening ceremony,
a televised frenzy,
plenty of electricity today,
so that everyone can witness
the irony.

Government funds were spent to construct
all those new sports facilities in the city,
but it's money that could have been used
to import protein
for millions
of hungry
citizens.

Old folks like Abuela wouldn't be diabetic
and nearly blind, if humans were valued
as much as publicity.

Storm Surge
Liana

My brothers immediately understand what I'm doing,
there's no way to hide all the black market deals
I conduct by trading things I find in the caves
for supplies to help rafters.

My life of secrecy suddenly feels like a storm surge
during a hurricane, swooping closer and closer,
pulled
     by whirling winds
that rise
from the heated

         sea.

For so long, all I've cared about was Amado and Paz,
but now my own family seems real again too,
hungry, needy, close,
desperate.

New Rules
Amado

As we watch the games, I hear official announcements,
learning that laws are suddenly changing, perhaps just
to impress visiting foreign heads of state
with a flurry of new freedoms for Cubans.

Churches are opened after decades of being shuttered.
Overnight, possession of a Bible becomes legal
and prayer
is no longer forbidden.

What will be next?
Permission to buy, sell, cook, eat?
Imagine how wondrous it will be
if Liana can open her daydreamed restaurant
and I am able to grow all the food we need
freely.

Boatless

Amado

The next time I go to the beach, I compare
our shore to other lands shown on television
whenever an athlete is introduced—distant places
with coastlines where fishing boats and freight ships
luxuriate like dolphins or whales, festive
and immense, gliding swiftly across
a peaceful sea.

We have hardly any boats at all.
It's our government's way of making sure
that no one tries to leave, not even when we're
starving, so we're captives, prisoners of hunger.
Some of the rules might be changing, but unless
they're altered swiftly, we'll be an island
of skeletons.

Tonight I'll find Liana,
I need to talk to her before it's too late
for words.

How?
Amado

no way to begin

so I wait for slow movement

my voice masked by smiles

Division

Amado   Liana

I miss   you
when we're   distant
we need   to share
feathers   wings
words
air

Unity
Liana and Amado

Our
hearts
know
how
to
soar
toward
each
other
this
turbulent
kiss
somehow
peaceful.

Refuge
Amado and Liana

Barracuda,
red snapper,
angelfish,
it's all the same
as long as we're fishing together
in a hidden cove, or trading together
in an alley at night, or cooking
together, in the cave's
farthest chambers,
surrounded
by possibilities . . .

but Amado says he needs to ask me
something important, and I'm afraid I know
what it will be, so I fall silent
avoiding
disagreements.

Visible Thoughts
The singing dog

The troubled dog watches as the boy
builds a raft in his mind
and the girl avoids seeing the drift
of complicated objects
that will soon be wrapped around her future,
each strand of salvaged rope
or splintered boards
one more
disappointment.

They'll leave him, won't they?
Should he abandon them first,
to make the flow
of human disloyalty
less painful?

Pain Relief

Liana

Amado, Paz, and I are still a team, bartering
and bargaining—but the dog seems restless,
Amado is evasive, and black markets are fickle
while ration booklets are tricky, since shoes,
cloth, needles, thread, and bed sheets all require
the same numbered ticket, so that in reality
only one
of those necessities
can be obtained
by each person
each year.

Aspirin, underwear, soap, shampoo,
paper, pencils, toilet paper—none of it exists,
the shelves of ration outlets are almost empty,
so when my mother awakens with a migraine,
all she can do is chew willow bark
and plaster fragrant sage leaves
onto her forehead, returning
to the remedies of ancient times.

She'll stay home from work today,
and I'll have no way to do any of my usual

exploration, I'll have to stay home
and take care of her, offering
the same comfort she always gives me
when I'm sick.

I realize
that this is what life will be like
                    in a few weeks
when Amado and I have to go back
to school,
                    and there will never
be
any privacy.

He keeps saying he needs to talk to me
about something urgent, but each time
I ask him to explain, he grows moody
and remote,
making me feel
so alone.

The Language of Wishes
The singing dog

The dog knows how uncertain the future can feel
while it still drifts a few minutes or centuries away,
so he tries to convey his canine sense of time
as a circle instead of a line, but his human friends
understand so little of his melodious voice
that he ends up guiding them with longing
instead of sounds.

Surely they will sense his need for complete
devotion, the kind that never doubts itself
even for a moment, because life spans
in the mind of a short-lived creature
are endlessly
fragrant.

Why?
Amado

My parents ask why I'm so gloomy,
a neighbor asks why I've gained weight,
a tourist asks why I'm so skinny,
a policeman asks why I'm evasive,
Liana asks why I won't just say
whatever it is that I've described
as terribly urgent.

Hunger separates people.
Fear does the same.
I'm afraid to share
my secret plan.
A raft.
The sea.
Escape.

What if Liana refuses to go with me?
What if refusing might save her life?
Can I imagine a future
alone?
   ¿Por qué?

Hunger Separates Siblings
Liana

I'm furious with Amado for failing
to trust me. Why does he keep secrets
when I'm more than willing to share
any burden?
Why?

After a summer of avoiding my parents
to prevent them from keeping track
of my movements, there's a part of me
that's so happy to see my brothers
at last.

We used to be close.
Now we're remote.
Why do they whisper,
sketch tracks in beach sand,
study the glaring horizon
of sunlight
and heat?

Time Travel
Amado

While Liana stares at her brothers,
I chat with old friends, then casually
wander the roadsides,
intent on convincing
the secret police
that nothing has changed,
no message was received,
no scribbled note
from prison.

A herd of bony white cows
is guarded by young men and women
in military uniforms, bodies twig-shaped,
faces haggard, eyes resentful.

Will that be me if I stay on the island,
just a soldier assigned to tend cattle
destined for restaurants in the city
where tourists eat like kings
while Cubans starve?

Food Riot
Liana

While Amado is out roaming on his own,
Paz and I notice women growing restless around
the ration outlet, some of them boldly pounding
    wooden spoons
        against enamel
            pots and pans,
as they shout
      ¡Hambre!
demanding
      groceries.

Hunger!
I shout too.
My brothers join me, bellowing
as they add the sound of stamping feet,
drumming their ragged shoes
against the sidewalk,
all of us risking arrest
for screaming such an obvious
truth.

Private
Amado

The food riot changes everything.
Police are suddenly everywhere.
City planners.
Government officials.
Every sort of bureaucrat
with the exception of those
who control food supplies.

A fence at the beach?
We've been banished?
An unwritten sign: Private. Exclusive.
NO LOCALS ALLOWED.

The fence needs no explanation.
We know when we're not welcome.
When I try to jump over, a soldier
chases me away.

Endless
Liana

There is no limit to the number of beaches
we can reach by hiking, but I long for the sand
where Amado and I consumed that first
seafood stew, behaving like merfolk
from a myth, the singing dog
our only witness.

Disappearance
Liana

As if losing our beach
were not enough turmoil
now my brothers have abruptly
vanished.

In times as strange as these,
some people become invisible.
Rafters.
Prisoners.
Fugitives.
They simply disappear,
leaving families confused
and desolate, like mine,
Mami crying, Papi raging,
Paz and I ricocheting
back and forth
between sobs
and silence.

Questions about Before and After a Disappearance
Amado

Were they arrested like my brother
or did they invent a haphazard balsa
like all those people in the cave?
I've longed to build a raft too,
but how can I face
such an uncertain future?

        Did they float away?
        Will they survive?
        Should we follow them
        or stay and search, in case
        their raft
        breaks apart
        and washes ashore?

What if
weeks pass
months
years?
What if
we never
know?

Search!

Liana

When family members go missing
the whole universe seems to vanish,
so we walk with Paz between us,
his nose on the ground sniffing footprints
that I can barely see through a mist
of tears and fears.

Amado

Streets, fields, beaches, caves—
just like so many other secrets,
the trail of a human
is found by a canine tracking
an aroma I can't detect, so I have to trust
Paz as he crouches at the edge of waves,
a watery endlessness
so impossible for humans
to truly understand.

Abandoned
Liana

They've hurled themselves into the sea!
No farewell, note or clue, no words or embrace.

When you live on an island that you're not
allowed to leave, each balsero who rows away
carries your wishes along with his own,
but when the rafters are your brothers
they take more, so much more
than daydreams.

The yearning they carry is solid and real,
like driftwood or sea glass, a wave-sculpted
monument
of grief
sinking.

Weary
The singing dog

The animal is exhausted.
He doesn't know how to protect anyone
from the devastation of history.
Hunger is a weapon that forces
strong young people to flee,
and now he's left with the sorrowful silence
of Liana's whole family as they crouch
around a radio all night, sleepless, listening.

The Names of Survivors Ride Back to Us on Air Waves

Liana

We lean close to our old Russian radio, press our ears
against empty air, and listen, listen, listen to voices
from Florida
reciting the names
of survivors.

We listen in darkness, because this foreign
radio station
is illegal.

The name of each rafter who has reached Key West
or Miami
is a blessing
for some other family
just like ours.

We know that if weeks pass
without hearing that my brothers are safe,
we can presume they've drowned
but we won't believe it, will we,
we'll imagine an unknown shore,

some place
from a map
of an imaginary land
like the ones in my mother's
old book of fairy tales,
a landscape with centaurs and unicorns
or children in rags who never give up
when they're assigned some impossible
magical
task.

Vigil
Amado

Liana is unable to sleep
or smile.

Even if I felt calm enough
to go out in search of food,
she wouldn't be peaceful enough
to eat.

As soon as the secret of her brothers' absence
is revealed to the police, her parents will be expected
to denounce their sons for breaking the law,
just as my parents were ordered to pretend
that they were ashamed of my brother
for his courageous
protest.

What If There Were Only Two People in the World?
Liana and Amado

Our embrace
      the only open spaces
                are gaps

shared breath
light
air

so that for at least one brief moment, we can
             rise
         far
           above
this sadness
and
fear.

Islanding
Amado and Liana

Anxiety all around us,
we isolate arms, eyes,
mouths

                    minds.

Together, we possess four legs,
like one creature
        earthbound
                sea-surrounded . . .

but we can't bear the thought of bringing a child
    into this time of hunger,
so we always
stop
short
        of creating
                new   life.

Dogs Know How to Wait, Wait, Wait
The singing dog

The loyal creature teaches them with his example.
Sit in one place, ears attentive, mind eager.
Expect your vigil to be rewarded with results.

Never let troubles convince you that you deserve
anything less
than absolutely devoted companionship.

Always be ready for life to bring a reunion.

Maybe Someday
Liana

Exhausting nights pass
with no news from the radio.

Daylight grows lonely, rain and sun
now identical in their ability to deliver gloom.

This effort of pretending to know nothing
about any rafters becomes excruciating
now that my brothers are the ones
who have vanished, forcing us all to act
normal, so that neighborhood spies
won't notice
and report us.

By postponing the inevitable discovery
of the twins' absence, we hope to give them
more time to float toward safety
without being pursued.

Maybe someday soon, I'll be able to smile or cry
freely.

Valley of the Nightingale
Amado

Flashlights with black market batteries
allow us to explore deep caves by day,
instead of just sitting around waiting
to mourn or celebrate
the way we do each night when we listen
to names that radiate like eerie moonbeams
from the radio.

Glimpses of tree roots help us know
that we're not too far from the surface.

Moisture drips down
through hidden openings.
An underground stream
leads to
bird songs.

We emerge from dark caverns
into a landscape of music and wings,
sound and color so intense that the voice
of each trilling ruiseñor
is like a wound healed
by distance, the vivid

green
of every palm frond
and grass blade
a promise—growth.

We could farm here.
No one would know.

We could hide here.
How much safer it would be
than floating across the sea
on a raft made of inner tubes
and desperate strands
of hope.

Valley of Silence
Amado

Safety is an illusion.
Any hidden refuge can be found,
and with my military service looming,
all I can offer Liana
is a shared determination
to keep our imaginations alive.

Resolve.
Invent.
Struggle.
Amar.

Love—it's that or build our own raft
and leave
our isla of hunger
forever.

Which should we choose, land
or sea?

Why So Quiet?

Liana

Amado's stillness
in our new valley of birdsong
is disturbing.

I imagine this is how it will be
if we ever decide to flee like my brothers,
with nothing around us but danger
and nothing inside us but fear.

Terror and wishes, the two
always seem paired in this time
of special starvation
or drowning,
an islander's
only
choices.

Fear in Two Voices
Liana and Amado

What if   if only
we float away   together
like brothers   like others
slow   swift
above a raft   below a raft
sun   waves
thirst   lungs
    such a vague chance
      arrival
      survival
      relief
      belief
      breath
What if
we stay
change
things
here
fear
if only . . .

. . . *What Would We Need?*
Liana

Sunscreen, fish hooks, compass, courage.

The army is voluntary for women,
but men have to serve in the reserves
until they're fifty, so if Amado stays here
he'll be trapped for nearly four decades,
half a lifetime, such a sacrifice!

Should he leave, could I join him, or am I
too cowardly to trade earthbound hunger
for saltwater
thirst?

He finally admits that this is the dilemma
he has been considering, the subject he's been
so reluctant to discuss, simply because
its possibilities are as vast and risky
as the whole universe, with countless
black holes and other incomprehensible
dangers.

Simple Verse
Liana

All we really need is one windblown week
to carry us beyond dreams of returning
so that arrival is our only yearning
no matter how distant the shore we seek.

Nothing Is Simple
The singing dog

Arms and minds entwined, humans forget
that even at sea, where waves offer rhythm
and rhyme, music is more than words.

Sound, sight, scent,
all the various aspects of air
blend and tangle in a way
that demands attention.

While Liana and Amado argue
about their future
all I can do is lead them
back to the edge
of wonder.

Nothing Seems Real
Amado and Liana

caves and beach
both feel imaginary
as we follow
a branched pathway
of uncertainty

questions
are endless—
what if
and
if only
both seem like something
more permanent than choices

undecided
we linger on solid land
wondering
which to embrace—rolling waves
or each other

At Last!
Liana

Just when everything
begins to seem as impossible as happiness,
the voice of a stranger on the radio
pronounces:
Sereno del Río Alegría
Segundo del Río Alegría

They've washed ashore near Tampa—
far off-course if Miami was their true goal,
but who can map the wind that drives an ocean?
Who can say that two full weeks
of sunburn, hunger, horror,
uncertainty, and deadly thirst
are not worth the risk
of arrival
survival
belief
breath
food
life?

Beachcombers
Liana

No more wishing.
My brothers are safe, and even though
our family is now marked by suspicion
of counterrevolutionary sentiments,
the global competitions are ending,
athletes will leave, and if any tourists stay,
they'll probably be fed by the government
on a private beach, in some air-conditioned
hotel restaurant
that hasn't been invented yet.

School, homework, uniforms, tests, hunger,
our future—if we stay—seems so grim
that with Paz beside me, I stroll along the shore
of an unfamiliar beach, searching for bits
of flotsam and jetsam that Amado and I can use
to build our own raft,
a magic carpet to float us away
from empty bellies
and hollow hopes.

Silence Is a Form of Protest
Amado

In order to keep their jobs, Liana's parents
are forced to denounce the twins.

They have to call their sons traitors,
but Liana assures me that she won't
do the same.

If a teacher,
secret policeman,
or neighborhood spy
demands the recitation
of some absurd statement,
she won't insult her brothers.

The people we love are simply family,
she assures me, not complex
inexplicable
historical
ideals.

Imaginary Rafts
Liana and Amado

Mi vida, my life, my love, ours—one, not two,
and yet somehow doubled—two, not just one.
We hold hands to decide whether to walk forever
on our island of hidden caves, eyes focused
on the aerial horizon
instead of dark depths.

Or should we risk
sinking?

We need this view of distance.
Imagine traveling on a ship or airplane,
such safety, sheer freedom.

All we have in our shared hearts
is one imaginary raft—
How should we use it?
Climb aboard or set it loose,
let that alternate future
drift away?

Discovery
The singing dog

Sniffing and seeking, the dog finds a tiny baby
left alone on hot sand,
helpless beneath scorching sun,
like a patient mirror of adult misery.

She's a startling sight,
wrapped so tightly in a blanket
that is far too warm for tropical weather,
like a bundle of dangerous secrets
in a black market vendor's sack of contraband.

Her dark eyes gaze upward,
risking damage from the powerful blaze
of intense sunlight.

Who would leave an infant
so close to the voracious ocean?
The dog sings to her, and she answers,
whimpering, then howling with gratitude
for canine sympathy,
the first step
toward human
help.

Abandoned?
Amado and Liana

The baby seems as isolated as an explorer
of some remote galaxy where gravity
does not tie
human feet
or minds
to solid
earth.

How can a parent leave a child
alone?

Do Humans Always Assume the Worst?

The singing dog

The infant's young mother emerges from the water,
her hands cradling the day's catch of shellfish
and seaweed, her hair as tangled as a mermaid's,
her eyes fierce as she reclaims her child,
clearly assuming that the odd-looking dog
might be dangerous
and the teenagers
are strangers
unworthy
of trust.

The dog licks the baby's cheek,
then the mother's hand,
in an effort to announce
that he means no harm,
and was only trying to guard the child
from loneliness
despair
pecking seagulls
hungry crabs. . . .

Possibilities as Vast as the Sea

Liana and Amado

We sing to soothe each other's fears.
The lonely baby is safe now,
the dog howls with joy, but how
can we be sure that what we hear
will not be transformed
into sorrow?

We Need to Live As If Time Does Not Exist
Amado and Liana

For one terrifying instant, the mother
must have imagined that we would report her
to dangerous authorities.

She could have lost her baby, even though
leaving him on the beach was her only way
to gather food and stay alive so she could feed him.

This entire island has been plunged into a dilemma
beyond comprehension, each of us choosing how
to divide up any scraps of edible treasures we find:
gobble it all ourselves, or save some
for our loved ones?

Gardening helps.
It's all we can do.
Share.

We need to live as if tomorrow
won't starve us.

Music of the Future
The singing dog

The dog senses he's in a time-shifting story
even before he hears a wistful melody
that leads him far away
from humans.

Someone heard his howl and answered.
He's not the last of his kind after all.

She's there, in that green refuge beyond dark caverns,
a mate, the one he's rarely encountered,
another remnant of the immense past, reclaimed, another
survivor.

His matchmaking work is finished for now.
The two humans are together, and they will be
the ones who decide how to live from now on,
while he will once again create
his own family, bringing hope all the way back
from near extinction.

Hope Is the Only Cure for Hunger
Amado

As soon as the baby is reunited with her mother,
Paz races away to find the source of howling,
while we stay on our new beach, determined
to think of this night as the start of sunrise
tomorrow.

I will not climb onto a raft if it means
taking a chance on being separated by death.

Imagine how lonely it would feel to be the only
survivor.

Imagine how lonely Liana would be if I
sink, and she soars.

We'll take our chances on hunger's shore.
We won't let the ocean
separate us.

Our Gardens Await
Liana

One kiss and fear recedes
like a tide, replaced by our love-driven
struggle
to learn
about
plants
soil
water
growth
nature.

In our hearts, there are two ways to be:
ser is forever,
estar fleeting.
When it comes to feeling free, we
need both.

Author's Note

Liana and Amado are fictional characters, but all the hardships they face in this story were real during the 1990s, when Cubans suffered near starvation. That decade of extreme hunger is known as el período especial en tiempos de paz (the special period in times of peace). Those who survived remember it with horror, afraid that hunger could return at any moment, depending on the whims of governments.

During the summer of 1991, after an absence of three decades, I visited relatives in Cuba, knocking on their doors unannounced, because I knew that islanders had been ordered to avoid interacting with foreigners who attended the Pan Am Games. I continued to deliver suitcases filled with food and vitamins throughout the decade when most Cubans grew emaciated, many suffering from diseases related to malnutrition. Shortages of food resulted from a combination of the sudden loss of Soviet aid; inefficient collective farming; bizarre laws that prohibited individuals from growing, buying, and selling agricultural products; and a brutal US trade embargo.

Throughout the 1990s, desperate islanders had to decide whether to stay and starve, or flee as refugees. Tens of thousands se tiraron al mar (threw themselves into the sea) on makeshift rafts, hoping to gain asylum in Florida. Countless balseros drowned. The names of those who survived were read over the radio, on Miami stations that were prohibited in Cuba. During one of my visits, I shared the excruciating experience of secretly waiting to hear the names of cousins.

Now, thirty years later, I choose to love the cousins who floated away from Cuba and became refugees, as well as those who stayed in their homeland, inventing solutions to daily problems.

Until the devastating 2020 global pandemic, hunger on the island had gradually decreased due to an increase in tourism, but most food was food still imported. Much of the protein is destined for tourists rather than locals, and staples such as rice and beans are still rationed. Small vegetable plots, street vendors, and farmers' markets have been legalized, along with paladares (home restaurants) and casas particulares (home bed-and-breakfast inns). The US trade economic embargo persists. In place since 1962, it can only be ended by an act of Congress. For readers who wonder about the blend of fact and fantasy in historical fiction, here are a few details that show how they can merge in a writer's mind:

—Cuba's singing dogs were described by priests who accompanied Spanish conquistadors beginning in 1492. I choose to believe that some of these indigenous canines survive, and I enjoy wondering whether they can serve as guardians and matchmakers.

—Cortés really did seize all the Spanish men of my mother's hometown as soldiers, and the enslaved indigenous men as porters for the conquest of Mexico. One mestizo named Uría refused to fight and was imprisoned. I descend from his Ciboney Taíno nation.

—I included a baby left alone on a beach because many years ago, I really did find one, wrapped in a thick blanket, beneath the blazing sun. I stayed with him until his young mother emerged from the sea with a meal fit for a mermaid. She told me she had no choice but to leave him while searching for food.

—El Valle del Ruiseñor (The Valley of the Nightingale) is reached by hiking through caves in western Cuba. For the purpose of this story, I moved it to the north coast near Playas del Este, from which most rafters depart.

Acknowledgments

I thank God for love and gardens. I'm grateful to my family in the United States and Cuba; to my dedicated agent, Michelle Humphrey; my wonderful editor Reka Simonsen; and the entire Atheneum publishing team.